MIDNIGHT
THE WITCHING HOUR

J. FALLENSTEIN

darbycreek
MINNEAPOLIS

Darby Creek
A division of Lerner Publishing Group, Inc.
241 First Avenue North
Minneapolis, MN 55401 USA

For reading levels and more information, look up this title at
www.lernerbooks.com.

Images in this book used with the permission of: © Hitdelight/Shutterstock
.com (graveyard); © iStockphoto.com/Ben_Pigao (football helmet); backgrounds:
© iStockphoto.com/AF-studio, © iStockphoto.com/blackred, © iStockphoto.com/
Adam Smigielski.

Main body text set in Janson Text LT Std 12/17.5.
Typeface provided by Adobe Systems.

Library of Congress Cataloging-in-Publication Data

Names: Fallenstein, J., author.
Title: The witching hour / J. Fallenstein.
Description: Minneapolis : Darby Creek, [2017] | Series: Midnight | Summary: "He
  seemed almost perfect. But when a girl finds out about the sinister ritual her crush
  plans to perform at the local cemetery, she has only hours to stop him"—Provided
  by publisher.
Identifiers: LCCN 2016024433 (print) | LCCN 2016037896 (ebook) | ISBN
  9781512427714 (lb : alk. paper) | ISBN 9781512431018 (pb : alk. paper) | ISBN
  9781512427912 (eb pdf)
Subjects: | CYAC: Ghosts—Fiction. | Dating (Social customs)—Fiction. | Horror
  stories.
Classification: LCC PZ7.1.F353 Wi 2017 (print) | LCC PZ7.1.F353 (ebook) | DDC
  [Fic]—dc23

LC record available at https://lccn.loc.gov/2016024433

Manufactured in the United States of America
1-41496-23357-8/30/2016

THE WITCHING HOUR

To my dad, who kept my brothers, their friends, and me entranced (and afraid to walk home through the dark) with his spooky tales. Dad, we never did find out just how you got away from the ghastly tall man in the old abandoned farmhouse . . .

CHAPTER 1

The car stopped abruptly and Rosie jerked forward, the seatbelt knocking the wind out of her. "Dad!" Rosie felt the welt that was developing where the seatbelt caught her shoulder.

"Sorry!" Her dad pointed to the dark figure that had just run in front of the car and darted into the thick bushes. "He came out of nowhere!"

Rosie glanced at where the boy had vanished. His dark jersey with the white 44 was still playing across the back of her eyelids. A heavy fog rolled off the graveyard and seemed to surround the car.

Her dad let out a sigh as he drove through the drizzle past a long line of cars parked on the side of the road. To Rosie's right, a few mourners in black wandered through the graveyard. Her dad pulled the car slowly ahead until they stopped in front of the ancient limestone church. Its Gothic wood doors opened, revealing six pallbearers carrying a shiny brown casket out of the church. They slowly started making their way across the graveyard lawn.

"Strange," her dad said. "I guess you don't need a hearse to get the casket to the graveyard if the burial is right next to the church."

Rosie peered more closely at the pallbearers: six boys about her age, three on either side of the casket. A shiver went through her. Man, she hated funerals. It had been three years since Jessica died, but sometimes it still felt like it was just yesterday. Rosie went from being a big sister to an only child. And then everything else fell apart.

Even though the doctors said there was nothing she could have done, she still felt like it was partially her fault. She had been home with Jessica; she was the one who'd been there the night her sister died. Why hadn't she checked on her sister just one more time? If Rosie had, maybe she would have seen her sister choking.

Rosie shivered and shut the vents on the dashboard. It was September, but the day was chilly. Many of the trees had already lost their leaves and were nothing more than dark skeletons.

The group following the casket walked solemnly in their dark clothes toward the open grave. The hair on the back of Rosie's neck rose. A creeping chill made her shudder.

"You all right, Rosie?" her dad asked.

She nodded. "Let's just get to your house so I can unpack." Starting over in Middleton meant that she needed to stop dwelling on the past, Rosie reminded herself. She took one last look back at the funeral and just caught the street sign as they passed: Zumbay Road.

Rosie didn't want to look at the sad sight of the mourners anymore so she flipped down the visor to check her face. She smoothed her hair. Man, her light roots were growing in fast, and the dishwater blond didn't look good with the rest of her bright red hair. But she hadn't had time to do anything but pack and say quick good-byes to her friends since her mom had announced her three-month transfer to Germany. Rosie basically had no choice but to move in with her dad, in Middleton. A town far enough away from everything and everyone to keep her isolated from her friends. But at least here the locals spoke English. She flipped the visor back up.

"I wonder who died," Rosie said as they turned down the next road. An unsettled feeling rose from the pit of her stomach.

CHAPTER 2

Three hours later, after a marathon unpacking session, Rosie was hungry. "Dad?" She poked her head into his study. "Hey, Dad, can we get something to eat?"

He pulled off his reading glasses as he leaned back from the computer screen. "I can't leave this, sorry. I'm in the middle of a live meeting. Why don't you head to Dina's and get yourself something?" He pulled the wallet from his back pocket and handed her a few bills. "Oh, and go to the hardware store to get yourself a key made."

"For the car?" Rosie asked. If it ever stopped raining, the little beige convertible would be a pretty sweet ride.

He handed her his keys. "Just the house for now."

"Okay," she said halfheartedly, putting the key ring into her purse.

Dina's was a diner in the middle of town. With only a few booths and a handful of stools at the counter, the diner wasn't very big, but it was comfortable enough.

"Sit wherever," the plump waitress said, waving a laminated menu at Rosie.

Rosie walked past the stools at the counter to a booth in the corner and plopped down. The cook looked up at her from his work, grunted a sound of acknowledgment, then went back to chopping onions. Rosie glanced around. She was the only one there.

"Where is everybody?" Rosie asked.

"People haven't been getting out much lately," the waitress said as she set down a glass of ice water. "You new here?" She pulled a pad and a pen from the front pocket of her white apron.

"My dad lives here. Bennet. Bennet Nett."

"Oh, Mr. N. Sure. You must be Rosie, the daughter he's always talking about." She gave Rosie a genuine smile. "Well, I suggest a burger. One, because they're pretty good, and two, because we're out of most everything else. Except pie. We always have pie." She motioned to the tiered plates of pie on the counter.

"A burger with everything on it and a slice of pie it is," Rosie said. "Do you have apple?"

"Sugar, we have everything," the waitress said before squeaking away in her white tennis shoes.

Rosie peered out the window at the deserted street. First Street was Middleton's "downtown" area, but it didn't amount to much. Next to the empty bus station stood an old brick hardware store. Farther down was the post office and Middleton High and then the grocery store. Then out near the cliffs on Zumbay Road were the church and the graveyard. That was Middleton.

If Rosie was starting fresh, then she would have to try to meet people. There had to be kids her age; there was a high school. Of course, someone had just died, and, given the age of all of the pallbearers,

Rosie had a bad feeling that the burial this morning was most likely for a teenager. The current circumstances didn't make it the most appealing time to be the new kid in Middleton, right in the middle of a tragedy. But she knew, maybe better than anyone, that everyone could probably use a good distraction. And she was more than willing to be that distraction.

A few minutes, later the waitress returned with the sizzling burger. Rosie swallowed the hard lump in her throat. Her stomach churned.

The waitress caught her eye and said, "You're looking a little glum. What's going on?"

Rosie shook her head. "I saw that funeral today. I hate to ask, but who was it?"

"Mackie. Mackie Blackwell. Really sad story."

"What happened?"

"He was out on Zumbay Road with a blown bike tire."

"Zumbay?" Rosie remembered the name. That was the street they'd driven in on. "The road that winds past the graveyard?"

"Same one. Except Mackie was about a half mile out, at the big curve over the ravine.

Around midnight he calls his friend Omar
to pick him up because it's starting to rain. A
big storm is coming. Omar drives to get him,
doesn't see him in the storm, and . . . well.
They found Mackie's body about halfway down
the cliffs."

"That's terrible." Rosie eyed the grease
puddle that oozed onto the plate from
the burger.

"Omar insists he didn't hit him. That
he never felt a bump or collision. He thinks
Mackie jumped out of the way—over the
guardrail—and lost his balance. But others
aren't so sure." She sighed as she poked her pen
into the dark curls piled on her head. "Either
way, the whole town's crying their eyes out."

"But not you?"

"I've done my share of crying." As she
said it, the lights caught her face and the
hard lines of years of worry became visible.
"Somebody's gotta go to work, and if my
husband won't get off his sorry butt, then
I guess it's up to me." She shrugged and
squeaked back to the kitchen.

Rosie took two small bites of the burger. She didn't feel very hungry anymore. The waitress returned a few minutes later with a piece of apple pie. She gave a disapproving look at the partially eaten burger.

"So," Rosie started. "Omar's responsible for his friend's death?"

The waitress nodded slightly and continued. "Tore those boys apart. Used to be the three of them: Mackie, Jack, and Omar. They were inseparable. Played football together since they could walk. In fact," she filled Rosie's water glass, "they even buried an old football with Mackie. It had their three names on it: Mackie Blackwell, Jack Blackwell, and Omar Arglos. Side by side. Kind of a pact that they'd be friends forever, I guess. But not anymore."

"Jack?" Rosie said sipping her water. "Who's Jack?"

"That would be Mackie's twin."

"His twin! Oh no. That must be awful."

"It is. And I can't say for sure, but since the accident—and I mean the whole month Mackie was in that coma—I haven't seen Omar and Jack together."

The waitress disappeared into the kitchen as the bells on the diner door jingled and a boy about Rosie's age walked in. He was thin, but he had the body of an athlete and walked with the dexterity of a cat. Shaved into the back of his close-cropped Afro was the number 44. Just like the number on the jersey of the boy who ran out in front of their car at the graveyard. He was lucky he didn't get hit!

As he made his way to a stool at the counter, Rosie tried to catch his eye, but he didn't so much as glance in her direction. This was it—her chance to make a friend before school started. She cleared her throat, but he just sat there. She coughed, but he kept staring straight ahead.

Rosie looked intently at the boy, who was mumbling something but still ignoring her. Drastic times called for drastic measures so she moved her fork to the edge of the table, gave it a little shove, and let it clang on the floor.

Still he didn't turn.

"Omar," the waitress said as she came out of the kitchen's swinging doors, coffeepot in hand. "I'm surprised to see you here."

Rosie gasped. That was him, Omar, the boy who everybody thought killed his friend.

"Didn't want to be home anymore and I got hungry," Omar replied.

"You didn't go to the luncheon?" the waitress asked.

Omar shook his head. "Jack was there. He told me . . . well, you know how he feels about me."

"It's tough," the waitress said. "You boys were so close."

The waitress poured him a cup of coffee and brought over a piece of coconut cream pie. Then she walked over to Rosie's booth. "How about you, Peaches, anything else?" The waitress pulled the pad from her apron pocket. Rosie lifted her water glass. The water on the table swirled and beaded into a strange shape. It almost looked like a tiny 44.

Rosie shook her head as she pulled her dad's twenty from her small purse. "Nothing else, but—" she touched the waitress's hand and whispered, "could you use this to pay for Omar's bill too? Don't tell him it's from me though. Well, it doesn't matter—he doesn't know me anyway."

"Sure, hon. That's sweet of you."

Rosie slid to the edge of the seat, taking one last bite of pie as she got out of her booth. She walked slowly past Omar, whose head was tilted like he was talking to someone next to him.

"I didn't see," he said. "It was dark. Should be me in that grave. Should have been me, bro."

Rosie looked around to see who he might be talking to, but there was nobody else in the diner.

An uneasy chill settled around her. She looked up at the air vent right above her, but it didn't seem to be on. She moved to the door. The glass on the door's window had fogged up and the words *Help him* appeared in shaky letters. Rosie gasped and spun around to see who could have written it but even the cook and the waitress were gone—there was only Omar at the counter.

CHAPTER 3

Rosie pushed past the smudged message and dashed out the door. A light rain fell as she headed to the hardware store. Her footsteps seemed to echo down the deserted street, and she tried to shake the feeling that someone was following her. She hurried under the faded Johnson's Hardware sign, looking over her shoulder as she ducked into the old brick two-story building. An antique metal fan blew a puffy, gray dust bunny across the wide wood planks of the floor. The shelves nearest the door and register were stocked with candy. A low freezer full of ice cream sandwiches hummed in the corner. Rosie spotted rows of household goods, mops, and a small display of nail polish, and she hoped that somewhere there might possibly be some hair dye.

A little arrow sign that said *Keys Made* pointed Rosie up the stairs. As she stopped in front of the key-making machine and dinged the small metal bell, a teenage boy in a red vest ran up the stairs, calling out, "I got it."

"I need a duplicate made." Rosie handed him the key to the house.

"Just this?" he asked.

She felt along the ridges of the car key. Maybe Dad would let her take the convertible to school the first week. There was no reason he shouldn't—he worked at home so he didn't need it during the day. Plus, a spare key was always a good idea in case of an emergency. "Um, this one too," she added, handing him the key to her dad's convertible.

The boy examined the car key and nodded, turning to spin through the shiny rack of blanks. "Old school," he said, giving Rosie an approving smile. As the machine sawed away at the metal, Rosie's eyes wandered around the store, looking for something to talk to this boy about. Maybe he could be her first Middleton friend. Her gaze went to the colorful poster on the bulletin board behind the counter. Under the headline "Benefit for Mackie Blackwell" was a large picture of Mackie in a dark number 44 jersey holding a weathered football. That number. It came to her in a rush: 44 was Mackie's number, not Omar's!

But then why did she . . . She shook the image of the jersey at the graveyard and the water beads on the table from her mind and concentrated on the photo on the poster. The picture was eerily familiar. Her eyes went to the boy working the key machine. He was the spitting image—if not a bit more haggard and thin—of the boy on the poster. Her eyes darted to the red letters on his white name tag: Jack.

She shifted uneasily. Mackie's twin right here in front of her. How could she make sure not to say the stupidest thing in the history of stupid things said?

Jack placed the two keys on the counter. "Anything else today?" He barely looked up.

"Dye."

"Excuse me?" His dark eyes flitted to hers.

"Dye? Do you have dye?" Did he think she said *die*? Her face burned. "I mean hair . . . color, for your hair, not *your* hair, but head hair, that grows . . ." She touched her roots.

"Jack?" a deep baritone voice called up the stairs. "One of your teammates is here to see you."

Jack flipped off the key machine. "Better not be Omar," he muttered. "Still can't look at that dude." An older woman with a mop of gray hair leaned out from behind the gallons of paint.

"Omar needs to leave you in peace." She nodded solemnly at Jack. "That Arglos boy has done enough damage to this town."

Rosie followed a few feet behind Jack. She held the railing as the balding, rotund owner of the deep voice continued, "It was an accident, Jack. You boys have been punishing yourselves enough over this. Cut Omar some slack."

On her way to the register Rosie scanned the beauty products for hair dye. But her face still burned from her stupid *dye* comment. A growing panic made her break out into a light sweat. She just wanted to get home, so she headed for the register.

Jack's friend was waiting at the door of the store as Jack checked Rosie out. A tall, red-haired boy. Clearly not Omar. He gave her a funny look and exchanged a glance with Jack as Rosie paid for the two keys. She didn't think now was the best time to try to introduce herself to yet another stranger after her utter failure by the key machine, so she walked as fast as she could past the boy, out the door, and headed home.

The waitress was right when she said the accident had torn Middleton apart; it was almost as if people were taking sides. No wonder Omar looked so worn out at Dina's. People *did* blame him for Mackie's death. Well, if there was one thing she wasn't going to do, it was sit by and let him suffer. The way people treated her after her sister died was terrible. Some people avoided her as though death were contagious. And she couldn't help but see the hints of blame in the sad looks from people who were willing to make eye contact with her. Then there were the people who came up to her crying, making her feel like she had to comfort them. No one, it seemed, could actually just sit and be with her—just talk. That's what she could have really used. Rosie thought of Omar. She knew what she had to do.

CHAPTER 4

The next morning Rosie got dressed, packed her backpack, and forced a brief smile in the direction of her dad as she headed out the door. She rubbed the new car key on her key ring. At least her dad had agreed to let her drive the car to school the first day.

As she pulled into the Middleton High lot, the day was already muggy and the convertible windows were fogged. In a few minutes it would rain.

Suddenly the temperature dropped, and a chill swept over her. The car moved slightly, as if some had just gotten in the backseat, but she saw nobody in the rearview mirror. Rosie checked the vents, but the air wasn't on. The heavy condensation formed beads that rolled down the rear window in streaks. It looked almost as if they were forming the number 44.

Rosie froze, remembering the poster at the hardware store. Number 44, Mackie Blackwell's number. She shook her head, trying to unsee the 44 now dripping down her back window.

She thought back to the dark figure that darted in front of their car at the graveyard. Rosie could have sworn that 44 was the number on the back of the jersey. But it couldn't have been because that would mean it was . . . Mackie who ran past her.

The car shifted again, and a draft like a cold breath blew over her neck. It was all officially starting to freak her out, so Rosie grabbed her registration forms, slung her backpack over her shoulder, and got out of her car. A lone figure ambled into the parking lot. Rosie caught her breath. He was thin, with an athletic build and short Afro: Omar. A real person, not a ghost. She let out a deep sigh. The wind whipped, pulling the registration papers from her hand, up, up, and then toward Omar.

Rosie scrambled after the sheets.

A few yards ahead of her Omar ran forward and swiped one sheet from the air and another from the ground.

"Oh my gosh," she said, her face bright red. "That was weird."

He handed her the papers.

"Thanks," she mumbled, tucking the wrinkled forms into her backpack. "I'm Rosie. Rosie Nett. This is my first day at school. I mean, not like *ever* at school. I wasn't homeschooled out on a remote island or anything. Not that there's anything wrong with that. I just, I mean, it's my first day here at Middleton." As hard as she tried, it never worked out; she was anything but cool. She forced herself not to sprint away screaming from embarrassment.

Omar nodded slowly and managed a smile. "I'm Omar, Omar Arglos." He gestured to her backpack where the registration sheets were now safely tucked away.

"I can see that you're new," he said. His eyes narrowed and then shot open in surprise. She turned to follow his stare, but there was nothing to look at but her streaked rear window. "Mackie," he whispered. "Not her."

"What?" she asked, "Not who?"

"You don't see . . .?" He pointed to the backseat of her car.

"I don't see anything . . . or anyone."

He shook his head and closed his eyes as if trying to get an image out of his mind. Finally he opened his eyes and said, "Thanks. That was nice."

"Okay," she said slowly. She was becoming more confused by the minute. "What was nice?"

"Buying me the coffee and pie." His dark eyes caught hers. "It's been some time since anyone was just randomly nice to me."

"Oh, I didn't . . ."

A small smile crossed his face. "You know that waitress can't keep a secret, right?" He motioned for them to walk to the school.

"Okay. I did. I bought you the pie." She walked alongside him.

"I bet it's tough," he said. "Being new here."

"Yeah, I'm a little nervous about being the new girl. Especially at lunch."

"Well, New Girl, forget about that. You're sitting with me. I take the table at the far end next to the windows."

Omar held the door for her, glanced back at her car, and then followed her in. He walked her to the registration office before heading to class.

***

The morning was a blur of new names and faces. But then came lunch and Rosie's heart fluttered as she headed to the cafeteria. Thankfully she already knew she could sit with Omar. As she got into the lunch line, two guys who had been in her chemistry class were talking in front of her.

"Man, without Mackie at running back, our team doesn't stand a chance this year."

The other guy, short and built like a brick house, shook his head. "Dude, especially with Omar out too. I don't know why we even bother."

Rosie took a tray as the first guy nodded his head in agreement. "What a loss, dude. Quarterback *and* running back both gone like that. We totally would have gone to state. Too bad Omar took Mackie out."

She slipped a piece of greasy cheese pizza onto her tray. Did the people of Middleton really think Omar was guilty? That he somehow wanted all of this? Poor Omar—he really was an outcast.

She walked through the sea of strangers to the table by the window. Omar smiled and shut his Spanish textbook—the same textbook she'd used two years ago.

"*Ya estás haciendo tu tarea?*" she said mischievously.

"What?"

Rosie laughed. "You're already doing homework?"

"Oh, *sí*," Omar said, stacking his flash cards. "You speak Spanish? Looks like I found a Spanish tutor!"

"*Sí*," she said. "But I can't promise any As." Rosie took a bite of the pizza. The warm slice was a welcome relief for her growling stomach.

A boy, gaunt and hollow-eyed, passed the table with his head turned away from Omar. As he sat down at the next table over, Rosie saw his face: Jack. Then another boy did the same thing, then another, until there were three of them at the table not even five feet away, ignoring Omar. Omar looked at them and grimaced, then looked out the cafeteria window.

"Why are they acting like that?" Rosie asked.

"Jack's never going to forgive me," Omar said. "You don't want to know."

Rosie paused for a moment, unsure what to tell Omar. She decided on the truth. "The waitress at Dina's told me about Mackie," Rosie admitted. "I'm so sorry."

He sighed and rain drops sprinkled on the glass. "It's okay. I had a month to think about it, every hour, every day that Mackie was in that coma."

She wiped the grease from her mouth. "I know he was your best friend. And I don't know exactly how you feel, but three years ago my little sister died. Then my parents couldn't deal so they got divorced. Everyone told me they were sorry and knew how I felt. But of course they didn't. No one really knows until it happens to them. I miss my sister so much."

Omar's voice lowered to a mere whisper. "Yeah. It used to be Mackie, Jack, and me. It was like we were triplets. They called me their 'brother from another mother.'" His eyes sparkled thick with tears as he covered his face.

Rosie sighed. "It's tough. Three years and I still miss her. But it does—I mean—it's not always as bad as it is at first," she said.

Omar let out a small laugh. "I had this football. And we were so serious about the game that when our football team took regionals in seventh grade we all signed that ball. We said that one day one of us was going to play in the NFL and that ball was going to be valuable. Then the two who didn't make it could sell it on eBay and live off that money."

"That's sweet."

"Yeah, we all knew it was going to be Mackie in the big time."

She glanced at the three jocks across from them. Didn't they see how badly Omar was suffering? "Was that the football you buried with Mackie? The waitress at Dina's told me about it."

He nodded. "That's the one." He turned to the window. "I haven't talked to Jack since." He let a finger trace the racing drops. "I didn't hit Mackie. I didn't even see him. How could I not see him? He had to have jumped out of the way. He just had to."

"Omar," she tried to catch his gaze. "No one blames you."

He turned back to her, his eyes narrowed. "New Girl, you really are new here."

They sat for a while in silence. Most of the other kids finished their lunches and left. A heavy pine scent wafted by, covering up the smell of greasy pizza. Rosie looked around for the source.

In a low whisper Omar said, "He's near, he's near." His eyes widened, his face filling with panic.

"What?" Rosie said looking around.

The warning bell rang and Jack walked past the table, turning his head the other way again, making it obvious he was ignoring Omar.

Omar closed his eyes and shook his head, as if trying to get rid of a terrible thought.

The ruts under Omar's eyes were deep. It looked like he hadn't slept in days. "It's okay," Rosie said and patted his arm. "No one is here." It was true, the cafeteria was nearly deserted.

"Let's dump these," she said after a minute, and they walked a few steps to the big rolling Dumpster. They came back to their table to find some of Omar's flashcards strewn across their spot. Omar shook his head, covered his mouth, and pointed.

"What is it?" Rosie's eyes fell to the three white index cards that lay in a line.

He turned wildly to her and said, "What does it mean?"

"Omar calm down." Rosie picked up the *Ve*, *a*, and *él* cards and stacked them. "Go . . . to . . . him? It means nothing, Omar. It's okay," Rosie reassured him, holding out the stack.

But Omar backed away from the cards, almost afraid of the small pieces of paper. He hurried out of the cafeteria muttering, "He wants me—he's trying to get me to the graveyard!"

"Omar," Rosie called, but he had vanished into the stairwell. She looked at the cards. It was peculiar how they had flipped up in an order that actually meant something. But was it more than just a coincidence?

CHAPTER 5

Rosie didn't see Omar the rest of the day. When she got home her dad took the car to run an errand and she sat in the silent house. *Ve*, *a*, and *él*—the words ran through her head. It really seemed to spook Omar. He acted as if it was a message of some kind. And the 44 on her car window. He'd seen that too and acted strangely.

That creepy feeling came over her. Rosie needed a distraction and the basement looked like it hadn't seen a broom in years. Maybe if she cleaned it up she could move her bedroom down there. It definitely had more space than her tiny room upstairs. She went to the kitchen and pulled the cleaning supplies out from under the sink. It was no wonder her dad hadn't cleaned in a while; he was out of practically everything. He was so focused on work it probably slipped his mind. Sometimes Rosie thought that even she slipped his mind. Not that her dad didn't care about her, but just that he was out of practice with the whole parenting thing. Rosie took a handful of bills from the emergency cash box in the kitchen.

The sky was overcast but at least it wasn't raining. She got her bike from the garage and pedaled down the street.

As she rode up the hill past Middleton High and the grocery store, someone was jogging up ahead of her along the side of the road. It looked like Omar. The shadowy figure disappeared over the top of the hill.

Rosie followed, pedaling down Zumbay, but the runner darted off near the church.

"Omar!" she called as she gained momentum. Even as she yelled out, the figure disappeared into the dark trees.

Rosie glided past the church's big Gothic doors and around the corner.

Someone was kneeling in front of what looked like a fresh grave.

"Omar?" Rosie whispered as she parked her bike next to the church. Slowly she stepped around a large tombstone, tiny branches cracking underfoot and a pine smell rising from the ground. She stopped.

Omar's voice was low. He seemed to be talking to the headstone. Rosie could just make out the name at the top of the stone if she squinted: Mackie Blackwell.

A light rain began to fall. The small back door of the church creaked open.

"Can I help you, Miss?" an ancient man in a black frock said from the doorway.

"No," Rosie said, shaking her head. "I was just . . . visiting."

The man clasped his pale hands. "Ah. Well. The dead like to know they're not forgotten," he said. "Your friend has already made himself at home, I see. Good, he'll like that." He nodded in Omar's direction. "I sense there is a bit of unfinished business."

Rosie turned to look at Omar. He stood at

the grave, arms around the tall granite.

"You could say that," she said and turned back to the old man, but he had disappeared into the church.

Rosie glanced back at the graveyard, but Omar was gone too.

***

At the hardware store Rosie pushed back the memory of the old man at the church and tried to remember where she had seen the cleaning products. She passed an aisle full of Halloween decorations: dark red chalices, fake spiderwebs, gruesome yard ornaments. At the end of the display Rosie found what she was looking for. She surveyed the household cleaner section before deciding on a toilet brush, some window spray, and a jug of all-purpose cleaner. On her way to the counter Rosie scanned the aisles for Jack, but maybe since he'd seen her sitting with Omar at lunch, he was avoiding her.

She pedaled home through the rain. In the basement, as she poured the cleaner into a bucket, a familiar feeling came over her. It was that heavy pine scent she'd smelled at the graveyard—the same smell from right before they found the flipped index cards. She couldn't shake the thought of what had happened at lunch as she got on her knees to scrub.

After two hours of cleaning, the basement sparkled. She managed to move her small dresser, rug, mirror, and clothes to the basement by herself. Now she just needed her dad to help her move her bed down.

Rosie's dad walked into the tidy room and gasped. "You did all this today?" he asked. Rosie beamed at him. After they moved the mattress, box spring, and bed frame downstairs, the room was done.

Rosie's dad surveyed her handiwork, clearly impressed. Now was the time to ask for a favor.

"You don't need the car during the day, right?" Rosie asked in a rush.

"I usually don't." Her dad glanced over at her, suspicious.

"So, could I maybe take it to school then? It's always raining, and if I walk I'll get soaked."

Rosie's dad thought for a moment. "Okay."

He nodded, eyeing the heavy rain through the window. "As long as you stay out of trouble."

She smiled. What did he mean by trouble? But it was better not to ask.

The next few days Rosie arrived to school early, ready to meet Omar and walk into the building together. But each morning she wound up disappointed. Rosie would sit in her car in the parking lot listening to the radio as she glanced through her chemistry notes, waiting until the last possible minute when she was forced to walk into school alone. She had hoped that meeting Omar would mean that she would feel less alone at her new school, but Rosie was starting to feel like just as much of an outcast as Omar seemed to be.

Finally, on Friday morning five minutes before the first bell, she saw him walking from the road into the parking lot. Rosie was relieved. Relieved that Omar was at school again, and relieved that she would have a friend back. She was tired of being alone and pretending that it didn't bother her.

"Hey, Omar," she called out to him.

He nodded at her. "New Girl."

"Got any plans this weekend?" she asked, giving his arm a gentle punch.

He shook his head no.

"One a scale of one to ten, how much would you want to go to the city to see a movie with me tomorrow?"

"Um, a thousand?" he said with a huge grin. All of the sadness seemed to melt away, and a genuine look of happiness spread over his face.

"But," his face dropped. "I can't drive though. Not after . . ."

"No problem," she said and motioned to the convertible. "Your chariot awaits."

The smile returned to his face as they walked into Middleton High together. *Great*, Rosie thought, *now all I need to do is to get Dad to let me take the car*. Rosie hoped that getting Omar out of town for a while might help him forget about Mackie and cheer him up. They talked about their favorite movies and decided that the third installment of the space war series would be perfect. Full of action. And nothing creepy.

CHAPTER 6

After some convincing and a promise to fill up the gas tank, Rosie's dad agreed to let her take the car to the movies. Rosie had a good feeling about the evening as she drove over to Omar's house. Omar had seemed genuinely excited about the prospect of getting out of Middleton for the night.

Rosie pulled up to the well-kept, white stucco house and honked. Omar bounded out of the front door, making it across his front lawn in six big strides. He threw open the passenger door. "Hey, New Girl," he greeted her.

She drove out on Zumbay Road, past the church and the graveyard. Omar stared intently out the window as if he were looking for something. Or someone. The memory of seeing Omar in the graveyard earlier that week flashed through Rosie's brain.

"What's out there?" she asked and immediately regretted it. Of course, his best friend was out there.

"Mackie. He was telling me to—" Omar broke off, thinking. "Maybe if I go . . ."

"Maybe if you go, what?" Rosie prompted him to continue, easing around bend in the road—the spot where Mackie fell. Omar went silent as he closed his eyes and leaned back until she was a mile or two past the curve.

"So, what do you think is going to happen in the movie?" she asked, changing the subject. "I heard they've already started filming a fourth one."

The next forty minutes to the theater seemed to fly by as they got into a heated conversation about the plot twists in the first two movies in the series, who was evil and who was good, and what it all really meant.

At the theater they took two seats toward the back. The previews flashed on the screen.

Omar smiled. "You ready for this?" he asked, raising his eyebrows in mock seriousness.

"Yes. Because I already told you how it's going to go down and you, *sir*, are going to owe me a piece of pie from Dina's." She smiled and poked his bicep.

"We'll just see about that," he said, sliding his arm around her shoulder.

"This is fun."

"Yeah, it is." Omar jostled her arm good-naturedly.

"You seem better."

"I've got a good distraction."

It was true, here at the theater Omar seemed more normal than she had ever seen him. He even gave Rosie a hard time about her dishwater-blond roots showing.

But then her stomach let loose a tremendous growl. Omar turned to her with wide eyes. "You eat a tiger today?"

She giggled. She'd been so distracted by thoughts of the weird things that had happened since she'd arrived at Middleton that she hadn't eaten all day. But it seemed like it was going

40

to be okay. Her plan was working! So now she needed a soda and some popcorn or she might just pass out, if not from hunger, then from pure exhilaration.

"Popcorn?" she asked. Omar nodded enthusiastically.

"I'll be right back." She stood with her purse and shuffled out of the row. The line for concessions seemed to take forever, and some of the soda spilled on her top as she navigated opening the heavy cinema door.

Rosie stepped into the dim theater. Someone was babbling, back to the left, near where she and Omar were sitting. "In that black jersey, I couldn't see you. It was night, bro."

She stopped. The vents hummed as they came on. The dark red curtains that ran along the wall rustled and billowed.

"Omar?" she called as her eyes adjusted to the dark. She took a tentative step towards their seats.

He turned to face her, eyes wide, his face glistening with sweat.

Rosie's heart thudded. "Who are you talking to?"

"You didn't see him?" Omar pointed to the curtains.

"See who?"

"Mackie. He was here. Just now. Coming for me." Omar shook his head, the rest of his rambling words too jumbled for Rosie to understand. The movie screen filled with light.

"Sit down, you're blocking the view," a man said gruffly from a few rows behind her.

Rosie slid into her seat next to Omar. She touched his arm. "Are you okay?"

"Don't you smell it?" Omar whispered.

"Smell what?" Rosie asked and sniffed. The normal movie theater smells of stale popcorn and sugar were gone, replaced by a faint pine smell.

"Mackie's forest fresh cologne. He always wore it."

"That's why you think Mackie was here, because of the pine smell?"

Omar shook his head no. "He was just here, Rosie. He came out from the curtain. I tried to explain. But he said I needed to go—to go to him—like change places I think. He wants me to go to the graveyard. At midnight. I need to . . ."

"I didn't see anyone," Rosie said as she glanced at the still-moving curtains. "Mackie isn't here, Omar."

The loud clash of swords filled the air as the movie started. Music and screams and the whir of flying machines filled the theater.

Throughout the movie Rosie glanced at Omar, but he stared at the screen zombie-like, barely blinking.

When the houselights came on, they both stood. Rosie turned to him. Was he truly so guilt-ridden that he was losing his mind? But he wasn't imagining all of it; she had smelled the pine too. What was happening?

"So, um, how do you feel now?" she asked. He'd obviously been seriously freaked out. But he hadn't bolted—he'd stuck it through. That was progress.

"Sorry," Omar said. "I guess I'm still dealing with it all."

"It's okay," Rosie said. "I understand. My mom . . . well." She didn't need to air all of the family's dirty laundry, did she? She didn't need to tell him about how her mom spent some time "recovering," as her mom's therapist called it, after Jessica died. Maybe it was enough that Rosie was standing by him while he got through this. She touched his hand and he grabbed hers. "Thanks," Omar said, as they walked out of the theater into the parking lot.

"I wish you would have known me before." He looked over at her.

"Oh yeah?" She leaned into him. "What did I miss?"

"Well, I actually had a pretty good sense of humor," he said. They walked through the cool twilight and passed a sleek, new SUV with a woman reorganizing some plastic bags in the car's open back. Her husband leaned against the side of the vehicle, holding her big, green purse.

"How's it going?" the man said, nodding to Omar and Rosie.

"Check it out," Omar whispered to Rosie and then turned to the man. "Sir," he began, "sorry, but in my humble opinion, that outfit requires a smaller purse, perhaps in a neutral tone."

The man shook his head, laughed, and repeated the joke to his wife. The wife's soft chuckle joined her husband's.

"See?" Omar flashed a grin at Rosie as she retrieved the keys from her purse.

"Does my purse meet the high demands of your inner fashion police?" she asked, holding up her fuchsia bag.

But Omar was standing statue-like in front of her convertible, staring at the bumper.

"Omar, what is it?"

His arm raised, a finger pointed to a red smear across the beige front of the car.

"You hit somebody!" he said and took several quick breaths.

"No, Omar, this must be from a cart at the store. Those red plastic carts?" She bent over and ran her hand over the mark. "See?"

Omar shook his head. "It's blood. He was here. Mackie. He was here." He gripped her arm, hard. "It was him. I told you I was talking to him in the theater. He's been following me.

He thinks I hit him. Killed him. But," a cry came from his lips. "I didn't. I swear." Tears fell from his eyes in relentless streaks.

"Omar." Rosie's hands found his shoulders. "Look at me."

Slowly, his gaze left the bumper and moved to her eyes.

"I didn't hit anyone with the car. Mackie is not here. It's okay. You're just panicking. I'm going to take you home now. Let's just get in the car."

Shaking, Omar got into the passenger seat. He was obviously traumatized and sleep deprived. If he didn't calm down on the way home she might have to detour to the hospital. He snapped on his seatbelt.

Rosie moved to her door and bent low. There was definitely something red on the car. But as she looked closer, even she could see that it couldn't have been from a shopping cart. The red smear wasn't a red shapeless blob—it was three words. Someone had scratched "Go to him" on the bumper. She felt a cold breeze on the back of her neck as she stared at the letters.

CHAPTER 7

As she pulled into the school parking lot on Monday morning, Rosie tried to think of an explanation for the red scratches on the car. She got out to examine the beige bumper in the daylight, and a jeep that apparently lacked a muffler rumbled in next to her.

Rosie kept her eyes on the bumper. Someone had definitely scraped those words into it. But why? She covered them with her hands.

Jack got out of the jeep. "Something wrong with your bumper?"

"It's just . . . ," Rosie started. "Someone scratched something into it."

"Let me see." And before Rosie could stop him, Jack pushed her hand out of the way.

They both stared at the bumper. Then Jack broke the silence, his voice level and low, " 'Go to him'? What is this, some kind of a joke? It's bad enough that Omar killed my brother, but to taunt me about it? And now you're in on it too?"

Rosie was stunned. She didn't know what to say. Omar taunting Jack? And Jack thought she was doing something too? "I didn't . . ." Rosie looked up at him. "What do you mean?" she managed to mumble.

"All the texts looking like they're coming from Mackie's old phone. I blocked Omar's number for a reason; I don't want to talk to the dude. So to hack into Mackie's phone to send me messages . . . It's nasty. Mackie was my twin. What Omar did . . . He needs to leave me alone. Writing '44' all over too. I don't know how he's doing it, but it's twisted."

"Writing '44'?" The images came rushing back to Rosie: the jersey at the graveyard, the condensation in the car, the water on the table in the diner. Rosie tried to keep her voice calm. "Look, Jack. I'm not doing anything to you and neither is Omar. Do you even know how hard this has been on him?"

Jack's eyes widened. "Seriously? How hard this has been on *him*?"

"I know Mackie was your brother, your twin, and I know what it's like to lose someone close to you, believe me," Rosie said. "But Omar is suffering too. He's suffering a lot. Did you think of that? Not only did he lose his best friend, his 'brother from another mother,' but it's like you and the whole town think he killed Mackie. Whether his car hit Mackie or Mackie jumped out of the way and lost his balance over the edge, it doesn't matter. It was an accident. A terrible accident. Don't you see that?"

Jack held her stare. "Of course I think of that. If things hadn't happened the way they did so much would be different." He looked up, blinking back tears. "But now it's like this. And it's all because one night Omar was careless."

"Jack! You don't even know if Omar hit Mackie!"

"Doesn't matter." Jack's voice shook with anger now, "He was careless and . . . he's the one living. He needs to pay for what he's done!"

And with that last outburst, Jack rushed into school.

Rosie stared after him, stunned. Jack had it out for Omar for no other reason than Omar was there when the accident happened. Rosie knew he was upset with Omar, but she hadn't thought Jack meant him any harm. But from the look on Jack's face—the anger in his eyes— it seemed like Jack would stop at nothing to make Omar pay for what happened.

Her mind went back to the day in the lunchroom. That deep pine smell. Could Jack have splashed some of that hardware store cleaner near the table when he walked by? And the Spanish index cards, her bumper . . . could that all have been Jack, telling Omar to 'go to him'—to die, just like Mackie had? It was so disturbing it was hard to think about. And now Jack was saying that Omar was pranking him, hacking Mackie's phone to send him texts. Why would Jack do that? To give him an excuse to hate Omar? But that still didn't explain everything—the number 44 appearing everywhere, what had happened in the theater. There was no way Rosie wouldn't have seen Jack if he was there. Besides, how could Jack have known about the movie in the first place?

The wind picked up, sending a chill over Rosie. The thick clouds threatened rain, and a low mist seemed to roll out from the trees to the lot.

The same creepy feeling she had in her car the first day of school came back. It was as if someone was watching her, following her. She tried to shake it off but it wouldn't leave her alone, so she gave up waiting for Omar and headed into the school.

***

At lunch Omar was completely zoned out, methodically taking bites of his burger and sipping his milk. Rosie tried to keep the conversation light, "Are there any good places to bike around here?" Omar continued to stare ahead, silent. She waved a hand in front of his dull eyes. "Omar?"

He slowly lifted his head. "Yeah, Geister Park has a trail, it's a little steep. Zumbay Road . . ."

"Great! Maybe I'll head out for a ride tonight if it's not raining. What are you up to?"

He shrugged. Thunder boomed outside the window and rain pattered against the glass.

"It's storming pretty badly out there," Rosie said. "How about I give you a ride home after school?"

Omar managed a small smile. "Sure, Rosie. Thanks."

After the last bell Omar strolled up to her car and tossed his backpack into the back seat. "Man, I love everything about this car," Omar said, running his hand over the convertible top. "I'm a total vintage fan. I was saving up to buy something like this before . . ."

"Yeah, it's a classic. Hey, do you want to drive it?"

Omar shook his head no and got in.

"Is it because you don't know how?" Rosie teased him as she started the car.

"I know how to drive a stick shift!"

"Really?" Rosie said as she started the car. "Shift for me then. I'll take the back roads so we don't run into any other traffic." She pushed in the clutch and Omar shoved the gearshift up to the left.

"Go, New Girl," he said, and she eased her foot off the clutch and gently pressed the gas. The car jerked forward and she gave it more gas. "Again!" she said, pushing in the clutch. Omar shifted down into second, then, as they drove further, up to the right, third, and then down into fourth.

"Now that you've got a feel for it, maybe you can drive this car for real sometime," Rosie suggested as she pulled onto his street. "If you think you can handle it."

Omar smiled. "I know how to handle a nice car."

"Good thing too. My dad would have killed me if we had gotten into an accident." Rosie pulled up Omar's driveway. He seemed like he'd relaxed and might be open to talking about Jack if she brought it up now.

"Omar." She turned off the car and touched

his forearm. "I talked to Jack today."

Omar nodded and pulled his backpack onto his lap. She looked into his eyes. "He thinks—and I don't think you are—but he thinks you're texting him from Mackie's old phone."

"What?" Omar's eyes shot wide open. "No," he said with conviction. "No, come on, you know that's not me."

"I know, but why would he say that?"

Omar just shook his head back and forth then flung the door open and got out. He put his head in through the window. "You know that isn't me, right, New Girl?"

Rosie nodded and he stepped back. "Thanks for the ride," he said, but his look was doubtful—like he wasn't sure whose side Rosie was on now.

She drove home. Why would Jack make up a story about Omar taunting him? What was really happening? There were three possibilities: One, Jack was actually making it all up about getting texts from Mackie. Two, Omar really was texting Jack by hacking Mackie's number. Or three, someone—or something—else was texting Jack and leaving the number 44 all over. A shiver ran up Rosie's spine. What if it wasn't option one or two?

CHAPTER 8

Friday night Rosie sat on the couch with her
chemistry book. All of her parking lot studying
wasn't going to fully prepare her for those pop
quizzes her teacher hinted at, and it wasn't
like she had friends to hang out with anyway.
She'd missed Omar at lunch since she brought
up Jack when she drove him home. Apparently
he'd stayed home sick for the rest of the week.
But Rosie wondered if it was really because
he was avoiding *her*. She'd just gotten settled
when someone pounded on the front door.
Rosie jumped up. It couldn't be her dad; he was
in the city at a meeting and wouldn't be back
until late.

As she peeked out her side window Rosie

glimpsed Omar's tall frame shivering on her stoop in the dark. She flung open the door.

"Omar!"

"I saw him!" he panted, his face full of terror.

"Saw who?"

"Mackie. He was, was . . ." Omar could barely get the words out through his shivering. "He was running in the woods along Zumbay, past the graveyard, near where *it* happened." A crazed look shot across Omar's face. He grabbed Rosie's shoulders, his eyes bulging, his face slick with nervous sweat. "He was trying to get me. Rosie, he was coming for me."

Rosie spoke calmly, trying to look Omar in the eyes. "Why do you think he's coming after you?"

"Because," Omar's voice was high-pitched like he was going to cry. "He wants to change places with me. He keeps telling me to go to him, but when I get to the graveyard nothing happens."

She put her arm around his shoulders. "Omar, why would he want that?"

A cry escaped his lips. "I don't know. Maybe I should have died. Maybe it was a mistake." He rested his forehead on her shoulder. "I would though, Rosie. I would change places with him."

"Oh, Omar, are you sure it was Mackie that you saw?"

He pulled back and nodded. "He was wearing his jersey. In the woods. Running in his cleats, keeping up with me. Pointing at his eyes, then to me, like 'an eye for an eye.'" Omar let out a wail and collapsed into her shoulder again. "This time I saw his face!"

Rosie's back buckled slightly as she tried to keep Omar standing. "Let's get inside," she said. "You sit on the couch and I'll get you some water."

She ran the faucet. How could Omar have seen Mackie? He saw the jersey, but the face? The only one who looked like Mackie was . . . Jack. She hated to suspect him, but how else could it be explained? Jack did say that Omar should pay for his mistake.

Rosie took the water to the couch. "Drink this." Shaking, Omar took the glass from her.

The rings under his eyes were like graves, deep and dark. "Omar, have you been sleeping?"

Omar shook his head and took a sip of water. "I try but I keep having this nightmare."

"What happens in the nightmare?"

He took a gulp of air. "I'm at the graveyard and Jack's there. He's throwing the football, but not to a person, to Mackie's grave." Omar put his hands to his face. "The ball keeps getting thrown back so I walk to the tombstone to see who's there, throwing the ball, and it's Mackie, dead in his coffin. But then his eyes open, except they're all white— no pupils—and he grabs me. Then I'm in the coffin and Mackie turns into Jack."

"Mackie turns into Jack?" Rosie repeated, confused.

Omar nodded his head. "Yeah, Jack and I are in the coffin and Mackie is standing above us. Only he's not letting us out and we start sinking farther and farther into the ground . . ." A shudder rocked his body and the water sloshed in the glass.

"I'm going to walk you home now," Rosie

said after Omar's breathing returned to a semi-normal rate. She took out a flashlight and locked her arm through his. Linked together, they slowly made their way through the misty evening to Omar's house. The moonlight glowed blue-white on the lawn. "Omar, why were you out for a run if you've been home sick?"

"I was rested. I got some sleep. But this . . . anxiety. I needed to move."

They walked up the steps. Inside Mrs. Arglos stood at the window, so Rosie left him at the door. "Get some sleep and try to relax," she said.

As Rosie walked down Omar's driveway a strange sound came from the trees behind Omar's house. She turned onto the road and shined the flashlight on the still, dark trees. Something moved, big and dark. Someone was hiding in the woods, watching Omar's house.

"Who's there?" Rosie tried to sound more confident than she was.

The trees rustled. Someone was there, hiding just beyond the beam of the flashlight.

"Cut it out! Jack, if that's you, stop this. Omar's been through enough." Rosie's voice shook.

The rustling stopped, but a breeze came out of the woods. As it passed by Rosie, a low hiss came from deep in the trees. It sounded like "Heeeelp hiiiim."

CHAPTER 9

Rosie raced home, slamming the front door
behind her as she darted through the house
locking the windows. She stayed up with all of
the lights on until her dad came home from his
meeting at midnight. Only then did she crawl
into bed and drift off into an uneasy sleep. Her
dreams were haunted by the hissing voice and
images of Mackie chasing after Omar and Jack.
Just after six the next morning her phone buzzed
with a text. Groggily, she pulled it to her face.

OMAR: Come over!

ROSIE: What's going on?

OMAR: He's here.

Rosie's heart pounded as she threw on
sweats and ran out the door. She sprinted the

three blocks through the cool, mist-filled morning. Lungs burning, she ran up to Omar's door.

The front door was wide open and Omar stood framed in its wooden arch drenched in sweat, shivering. As she stepped over the threshold, the strong smell of pine hit her nostrils.

"Where is he?" she panted as she walked into the dim house and closed the door behind her.

"He was just here," Omar said, his lips trembling and goose bumps covering his body.

"Mackie?" Rosie asked, but she already knew. Omar nodded. "What happened?"

"I woke up early," he said, his face gray. "It wasn't even light out, but someone was outside my window, whispering my name—hissing it—over and over. I thought it was a dream at first. But it wouldn't stop, so I rolled over and looked out." His hands went to his face. "It was Mackie. In his jersey, sweats, and cleats."

"Omar," Rosie said softly. "Mackie's dead. He can't have been outside your window."

But even as she said it, she didn't know if she completely believed it. Rosie sank down to sit on the couch. Something was definitely wrong. Someone, or something, had been behind Omar's house last night, in the dark trees, and had whispered to her.

"I know. And I tried," he said as he sat next to her, his voice wavering. "I tried to shake it off, convince myself it didn't really happen. Last night I took the medicine my doctor prescribed to help me sleep and I thought I was hallucinating. I know that's a possible side effect."

A wave of relief washed over Rosie. That would explain it. "You probably were, Omar. Or dreaming. It could have just been a really vivid dream," Rosie said, but even as she did she heard the hissing voice again, this time stronger—more insistent—coming from somewhere in the house.

"Help him!"

She sat up and slowly looked around.

"But when I came downstairs," Omar said, "both the front and back doors were wide open." He raised his eyes and looked straight at her. "Rosie, I locked those doors when I went to bed last night. Then I found . . . He left his number. He was here."

Rosie froze. "He left his number?"

Omar nodded and led her to the kitchen table where sheets of homework, books, and flashcards lay in a messy heap. Sitting next to the pile were pencils arranged in a number: 44.

Rosie stared at the pencils, unable to move. There was no way that was a coincidence. She tore her eyes from the table to look at Omar.

"I need to go to him," Omar whispered. "At midnight. That's what Mackie said. Midnight at the graveyard. Go to him."

Rosie tried to hide her horror. She surveyed the quiet house. "Where are your mom and dad?" she asked softly, her heart in her throat.

"Visiting Gram. They left last night."

She nodded and turned her back to the table, blocking Omar's view of the pencils. "Omar, you can't go to the graveyard. You don't even know what all of this means."

"He won't leave me alone until I go to him," Omar sputtered.

"But—go to him? How?"

He still isn't thinking clearly, Rosie thought. *He can't see how crazy his thoughts are. The guilt has finally taken its toll.* But as hard as she tried, Rosie couldn't convince herself that even she hadn't heard the hissing voice the night before and then again just now. All she knew was she needed to keep Omar away from the graveyard. She needed to prevent him from doing whatever it was he thought he needed to do.

"You didn't sleep, and you're obviously upset," she said. "Let's go lie down for a while." She led him to the couch. She couldn't leave him like this—maybe he needed to go to the hospital. "When are your parents going to be home?"

"Noon. Around noon," he mumbled as he reclined. She covered him with a blanket. The circles under his eyes were deep, his face drawn. In fact, he'd been looking rather gaunt these last few days . . . had he been eating?

"Try and get some sleep," she said, and he finally closed his eyes. She went into the kitchen, pacing back and forth in front of the table. In one quick motion Rosie shoved everything back into Omar's backpack.

The wind blew and a breeze came through the house as if a door had opened. Rosie sat down at the table. In the other room Omar mumbled, as if talking to someone in a dream, "The graveyard at midnight . . . I will take your place . . . your grave."

Rosie got up and walked to the couch. "I'll stay here until your parents get home," she said softly once his mumbling finally stopped. She walked through the house to look out the windows on the back door.

All along the hallway, from the front door to the back, were dime-sized clumps of brown dirt. The kind of clumps that fall off cleats. Suddenly Rosie thought of Jack's anger. Jack. He must have been staking out Omar's house, waiting for him to be alone.

Rosie kicked a clump of dirt. Jack probably laid out the pencils too. But that didn't explain the voice—the hissing—she'd heard. That couldn't be Jack. The voice was unlike any human voice she'd ever known.

She pushed the thought aside. Maybe it was Jack. But if Jack was willing to break into Omar's house to torment him while he slept, when would he stop?

CHAPTER 10

Omar's parents came home while Omar was still asleep on the couch. "Mrs. Arglos," Rosie said. "Omar's been . . ." Rosie didn't know exactly what had happened, "having hallucinations," she settled on. "Could it be his medication?"

"Yes. I should have considered that." Mrs. Arglos turned to her husband. "We have to get him off it. No wonder he's been acting strange." She gave her husband a significant look as she left the room, prescription bottle in hand, to call the doctor.

Once Mr. and Mrs. Arglos were back to keep an eye on Omar, Rosie marched down the street with her sights on the hardware store. She would tell that Jack Blackwell a thing or two about his twisted vengeance. Rosie was almost certain it had to be Jack. She had spent the entire time Omar was sleeping working out how Jack could have done this to Omar. It was time to confront him.

Rosie pushed open the door to the shop and headed up the stairs. Jack was busy cutting a key. His shoulders were hunched; his eyes were sunken wells. The prank was obviously taking its toll on Jack too. He turned off the machine. His movements were slow, as if he were covered in thick syrup.

"Jack," Rosie said and stepped toward the counter. "You need to stop."

He looked up at her, his dark eyes weary. "Stop what?" he asked with a yawn.

"This messing around with Omar, whispering to him at dawn outside his window," she gestured to the key machine, "making duplicates of his house key and going through his house opening his doors. And the pencils, number 44? That's creepy."

Jack scrunched up his face like he'd just smelled a rotten corpse.

"Yeah," Rosie continued, tapping her foot, "The pine smell was a nice touch." She waved her hand in the direction of the cleaning products. "But you shouldn't have worn your cleats this morning. The clumps of dirt gave you away."

He shook his head. "I'm not doing anything. I've been at work since five this morning unloading the new stock." He nodded to the shelves full of winter shovels and bags of salt. "I swear I wasn't over there. But you tell Omar that he can stop with the texting and the *go to him* messages all over. He needs to cut it out or there will be serious consequences."

"Sending you messages? Jack, I told you he's not doing any of that. I even asked him. He's not. I don't know why you'd say that, except maybe to cover your own tracks. He's messed up, for sure, but not like that. He's so delusional with guilt he thinks he's meeting Mackie at the graveyard at midnight tonight."

Jack seemed to wake up. "Really? Omar's meeting Mackie? What does he plan to do when he meets him?"

Rosie shook her head. "He seriously thinks he can trade places with Mackie! Jack, he would rather die than live like this, with you and the town all blaming him for what happened—for what was obviously an accident."

"That so?" Jack raised his eyebrows. "So full of guilt is he?"

"Yes." Rosie slapped her hand on the counter.

"We'll see about that," Jack said and disappeared into a back room.

***

The sky rumbled. Rain was coming. The gray bank of clouds hung oppressively on the edge of the horizon. Rosie's stomach growled. She might have just enough time to grab a bite and get home before getting drenched. The red flashing letters of Dina's lit up the dark afternoon as she walked into the little diner.

The bells jingled and the other customers looked around. Rosie made eye contact with the father of the family in the far booth and nodded at the two farmers at the counter who spun to glance her way.

"Look who's back," the waitress said cheerily. "You here for another burger? I know you liked it last time." She flashed Rosie a smile.

"I think I might have some chicken noodle soup," Rosie said and collapsed into a booth near the window.

"Coming right up." The waitress plucked the pen from her pile of curls and wrote on her pad.

Outside the clouds seemed to drop from the sky. The whole street grew dim. Rosie could barely see ten feet out the window. As the waitress placed a steaming bowl of soup in front of her, the bells jingled again and Omar dashed into the diner.

"I hit him!" Omar cried. "I hit him! Somebody help!" He rushed back outside.

Everyone jumped up at once and followed Omar out the door, through the heavy mist, to the curve of Zumbay Road. "There." Omar pointed to something dark in the tall grass in the ditch. Lightning flashed and the street grew almost as dark as night.

A crowd gathered as one of the farmers strode cautiously down into the ditch. He leaned forward.

"What you hit, son," he said, as he heaved a dark object up from the side of the road, "was the Johnsons' garbage can." The farmer set the brown can on the road.

The 44 painted on the can did look like the numbers on Mackie's old jersey, but it was still clearly a garbage can.

Omar turned to Rosie. "I swear I thought . . . am I going totally crazy?" he asked in a voice no louder than a whisper.

She put her arm around his shoulders. "No, Omar, no."

"You okay to get home, Omar?" the waitress asked as the crowd dispersed. Rosie eyed Omar's car. "I'll drive him."

She walked with Omar to the idling car at the side of the road. He lumbered around to the passenger side. Once they were in the privacy of his car, Rosie turned to him. "What were you doing driving?"

"My prescription. The doctor made me a new one that isn't as likely to lead to hallucinations." He pulled the orange plastic vial from his pocket. "I just picked it up."

His chest heaved, but his voice was controlled. "I thought, well, when we drove the other day I felt all right. And since it's only a mile to the pharmacy I thought I would try to do it myself, and then . . . " he motioned to the garbage can. "It just looked like him," he said meekly and looked down at his hands. "The whole town saw me," he said. "They all think I'm nuts."

"They don't think that, Omar," she said, pulling from the shoulder onto Zumbay Road. *At least the doctor is aware of Omar's hallucinations*, Rosie thought. *Now maybe with the new medicine Omar will stop seeing and hearing things. And maybe without Omar on edge things will calm down for me too.* Her lack of sleep the night before and Omar's panic had probably made her think she had heard the hissing voice too.

But Omar's behavior *was* getting worse. He really did think he was seeing Mackie. He even made a deal with him to meet him at the graveyard.

CHAPTER 11

For the rest of the day Rosie paced, wondering if Omar was all right, hoping the hallucinations would stop, and hoping he would go to bed and stay there.

But what if he did go to the graveyard? Was it really Jack who was behind all of this?

Jack. It had to be him. That was the only reasonable explanation, wasn't it? Maybe he had always been jealous of Omar. Or maybe he wasn't before, but Mackie's death had pushed him over the edge. Everything fell apart for Jack; he lost his brother and, on top of that, the death broke up the friendship of boys who were practically triplets separated at birth.

Rosie opened her computer browser and searched for the Mackie Blackwell fundraiser. The happy eyes of Mackie Blackwell stared back at her. In his hand he clutched the worn football—the three names, Mackie Blackwell, Jack Blackwell, and Omar Arglos, were just visible under his fingers. The same football that they buried with Mackie.

There were other photos. The three boys playing in the sprinkler with an orange foam football when they were probably in kindergarten. The three boys building a snowman—the snowman, of course, clutching a football. And then birthdays, junior high games, and prom pictures. Jack was in all of the shots alongside his two best friends. No, it didn't seem like he was jealous of Omar and Mackie. It really did appear that they were three of a kind.

Just after six Rosie picked up her phone. Should she call Mrs. Arglos and make sure Omar was okay? Rosie had hoped that he would get some sleep and then text her. Maybe she just needed to be patient. The last thing she wanted to do was wake Omar up if he was finally sleeping.

At eight she checked her phone again. Still no texts from Omar. Finally at eleven she texted him.

ROSIE: Hey, how are you doing?

No response.

The trauma and the medication. Could there be any other explanation for Omar's bizarre behavior? And why wasn't Jack dropping the story of Omar harassing him with texts? Messages that were sent from Mackie as if Mackie really had come back. She thought of the hissing voice telling her to "help him" and shivered.

What if Omar was still planning to meet Mackie tonight? If that was the case, she couldn't let Omar go alone. She looked at the time on her phone. It was eleven thirty. If she left now she would be able to stop whatever was going to happen at the graveyard at midnight. But she would have to hurry. Rosie grabbed a flashlight and slipped out the front door, slowly pulling it closed until it clicked.

The moon shone from a black sky as she hurried down Zumbay Road. A rolling fog filled the ditches and partially covered the road. Rosie looked back, but even the lights at Dina's Diner were off. There was no one else around; no one to help her if she found something horrible at the graveyard. She walked a little faster.

Ten minutes later she stepped onto the damp grass of the graveyard. Ahead, back near the forest of dark trees that grew behind the church, a shadowy figure stood in front of a small yellow light. He was there, at Mackie's grave.

"Oma—" she started but then stopped. No, she wouldn't call out to Omar and let him know she was there. Instead she hurried to the far right, into the trees. Rosie would sneak up on him and see what was really going on.

Her feet crunched on the dry leaves as she slowly made her way in the blue moonlight through the thick trees. The mist dissolved and Omar came into focus as she crept closer. He stood at the tombstone, holding a single candle. On the tomb was a familiar red chalice. Omar lifted it, as if to drink.

She needed to stop him. "Omar?" Rosie called loudly. He turned in her direction.

Something snapped up ahead of her in the trees and her eyes barely caught the white 44. "Hey!" she shouted. But whoever it was disappeared into the thick forest.

CHAPTER 12

"Stop!" Rosie yelled and ran after him. "Jack, is that you?"

She pushed the button on her flashlight and held the bright beam pointed in front of her. She ran after the numbers all the way to the end of the graveyard, to the sharp bend in Zumbay Road until the dark figure disappeared . . . right over the cliff.

"Jack!" she screamed and ran to the guardrail. Her heart pounded as she stepped to the edge of the road and shined the beam down. But the jutting limestone cliffside was empty. She'd lost him.

Rosie looked down at her phone. It was 11:58. She needed to get to Omar before midnight! Panting, she turned around and sprinted back to the graveyard.

Omar stood, staring into the woods, holding the now empty chalice.

"Omar," she said as she rushed up to him.

He held up a hand to block the bright beam of her flashlight. A line of dark red liquid ran down from the corner of his mouth and a slight smile formed on his face. He'd drunk it, whatever was in that cup. Rosie was too late to stop him.

"Why?" she asked. Omar nodded to the tombstone.

A note lay on the gray granite under the small candle. She picked it up and read: "Drink from this chalice and you will take Mackie's place."

Omar turned to look at Rosie with tears falling down his check and said, "It's all better now. I drank it."

Rosie grabbed the glass and sniffed. "What did you drink?" The faint tart smell was familiar. A cry escaped Omar's lips and he moaned as he collapsed over Mackie's headstone. "You forgive me, right bro? You forgive me. It's all okay now." He wound his arms around the stone as if to embrace it.

"Omar," Rosie said and pulled at his sweatshirt. "Omar, what did you drink?" But he only grabbed the stone harder.

"You were right," Jack said, standing up from behind an ornate gravestone a few feet away.

"It *was* you?" Rosie cried, pointing her finger at him. "You did this? What did Omar drink?"

"It was just cranberry juice. It won't hurt him. I just . . . I had to know," Jack said and took a few steps forward. He shoved his hand onto the front pouch of his red hoodie. His eyes softened as they went to Omar's face. "Looks like he really would change places. I guess he's not the one sending the texts . . . the other messages."

"Of course not." Rosie moved between Jack and the weeping Omar. "I told you that." She dropped the flashlight down at the base of the gravestone and leaned close to Omar's ear. "It's okay Omar; it's all over."

"It is?" Omar asked and let out a sob.

"Yes."

"I just didn't know who could be doing that stuff to me," Jack said. His eyes flashed to Rosie's.

"I was wrong. I'm sorry, Omar." Jack took another step and gently put his hand on Omar's back. "Omar, it's all okay now." He pulled at Omar's shoulder.

"It's okay?" Omar asked and leaned back from the tombstone.

"Yeah." Jack held out his hand to help Omar stand. He turned to Rosie, "Help me get him to my car. I'll drive him home."

"I can't believe you put him through this." Rosie grabbed Omar on one side as Jack put Omar's arm around his shoulders and led him through the dark graveyard.

Rosie stopped at the edge of the grass. Jack had parked across the road. How had she missed his car? Jack opened the passenger door to help Omar in and then shut the door.

"Was it you from the beginning?" Rosie asked as Jack walked around the front of the car. "All those horrible pranks?"

Jack shook his head. "I didn't do anything."

"You call this not doing anything?" She spread her arms open.

Jack nodded. "Okay. I *did* do this. But you came to the hardware store and told me he was going to be here, that he was meeting Mackie. If he was meeting my brother, I wanted to be here too. You said he would change places with Mackie, and now we know it's true. Now we know it was an accident and that Omar wasn't the one doing that crazy, freaky stuff to me."

"What stuff?"

Omar slumped forward in the front seat.

"*Go to him, go to him*, it was driving me crazy," Jack said as he walked around the car. "But I guess he was just wracked with guilt, like I was. I just needed a sign, some proof, that's all. And now I got it."

Rosie stopped and shivered, suddenly cold. If Jack was *really* getting those messages too, then why would he be doing the same thing to Omar? So who was sending them and doing all of the other crazy stuff that had happened?

At the lunch table, at the movie theater, at Omar's house?

Omar raised his head and looked out the window. "I did it. I put his soul at rest. Mackie's okay. He didn't take me with him." He smiled. "I know, Mackie. I did what you said. You were right. I went to him. We'll be all right now. That's all you wanted, wasn't it? For us to be together again. To be friends again. Thanks for telling me, Mackie. Thanks for making sure we would still be there for each other even after you were gone. You can go." Omar was rambling, staring at a spot just behind Jack and Rosie.

"I'll take him home," Jack said. "He obviously needs some rest. Do you want a ride?"

Rosie shook her head so Jack got in his car and drove off.

Rosie started following the car down Zumbay Road. Jack had sure worked hard to set this up, running through the woods in the jersey then circling around and changing into a red sweatshirt. Rosie took a few steps down the path that led to her house, squinting ahead.

As she tried to make her way through the dark, Rosie remembered her flashlight. She turned back to the graveyard.

The mist rolled in and for a moment the graveyard was shrouded in white. The candle went out as if someone blew on it. Rosie strode through the grass, batting her hands in front of her so as to avoid tripping on a tombstone. The cold, wet dew hit her ankles and sent a chill through her whole body. She sighed as she glanced at the red chalice on the ground. It was probably from the Halloween display at the hardware store. As she made her way to Mackie's grave, Rosie was still feeling uneasy. Suddenly, something moved behind her and she stopped.

"Hello?" she called softly. Her voice seemed to echo in the empty churchyard.

She scanned the gravestones to see if Jack and Omar had come back. The wind moaned as it blew through the cracks in the church walls, and the mist dispersed, revealing an empty graveyard. But she could swear someone was there, moving closer to her.

Rosie stepped up to Mackie's tombstone. A pungent pine smell hit her nose.

Something small sat near her flashlight at the base of the tombstone, gently rocking back and forth, as if someone had just set it there.

She bent and picked it up. The football was old, worn, and dirty, but the three names on it were still clear: Mackie Blackwell, Jack Blackwell, Omar Arglos.

"Mackie?" she said.

The dark trees rustled and a whisper hissed through them, "Goodbye, Rosie."